Buffy

VAMPIRE SLAYER™

the Dust Waltz

Buffy THE VAMPIRE SLAYER™

the Dust Waltz

based on the television series created by JOSS WHEDON

written by dan brereton   pencilled by hector gomez

inked by sandu florea

coloured by GUY MAJOR   lettered by ken bruzenak

editor SCOTT ALLIE

assistant editor BEN ABERNATHY

book designer KRISTEN BURDA

publisher MIKE RICHARDSON

executive vice president NEIL HANKERSON
vice president & controller ANDY KARABATSOS
director of editorial RANDY STRADLEY
director of production & design CINDY MARKS
art director MARK COX
computer graphics director SEAN TIERNEY
director of sales & marketing MICHAEL MARTENS
director of licensing TOD BORLESKE
product development DAVID SCROGGY
director of m.i.s. DALE LAFOUNTAIN
director of human resources KIM HAINES
general counsel KEN LIZZI

special thanks to DEBBIE OLSHAN AT FOX LICENSING &
DAVID CAMPITI AT GLASS HOUSE GRAPHICS

Published by
Titan Books Ltd
42-44 Dolben St
London SE1 0UP

First edition
October 1998
ISBN: 1 84023 057 6

10 9 8 7 6 5 4 3

Printed in the UK by the Bath Press

if i'd *lived* in sunnydale

as a teen, I'd like to think I'd have fit right in with Buffy and her pals. But the reality is, I'd probably have been no help at all. I would have crumbled in the face of vampires, werewolves, and probably mummy princesses, too. I'd be the biggest wussy in Sunnydale and probably end up vampire-chow before I reached my junior year.

Why?

I was so afraid of the dark as a kid, it was pathetic. So pathetic that now as an adult, I not only draw and write stories about monsters creeping around in the darkness for a living, but I'm a total sucker for stories that deal with the same, whether they be movies, novels, comics, or even TV shows...

...Well, if such a TV show existed, that is.

I'd long since given up on the idea of finding a show that would really satisfy my need to see monsters prowling around, hear them talking and growling, and being slain by cute teenagers. There just weren't any shows on the tube like that, so I was a poor slob, content with shows like The X-Files, and stuff that really never nailed it for me. In the meantime, I did my best to create stories of my own that dealt with monsters prowling around in the dark. I've come to believe that being afraid of the dark as a pip–squeak actually paid off somehow. But still, there was nothing on TV that I could totally dive into as a monster fan.

Then, one night in later summer of '97, my kids and I discovered Buffy the Vampire Slayer. The TV show. They were airing two episodes over two nights, in preparation for the upcoming new season. We couldn't believe it; there'd been a whole season of this stuff and somehow, we'd missed it! We huddled around the set and watched "The Witch" episode, and we loved it. I'd always had a soft spot for the Buffy movie, but this was so different. It was hipper, funnier, and the special effects looked much too cool for a TV program.

And it was scary.

It was like a gift had been bestowed on all four of us. From that point on, the kids and I have continued to watch Buffy religiously. I can't think of a better series that so completely encapsulates my love of the dark, embracing the creatures that inhabit the night. Buffy doesn't hold back or try to rationalize monsters and the supernatural as other shows do. It doesn't "camp it up." Buffy and her pals are comfortable with the idea that their town, as pleasant as it may be most times, is rife with monsters.

I can't think of too many things cooler than that to watch on TV. And I can't think of a television program that cries out louder to be explored in the medium of comics.

So it was natural for me to claw my way to the front of the line, or as near as I could get, to be involved with the Buffy comic-book experience. I had to get me some of that, and I knew I spoke the same language as the show does. I know the "the wiggins" well.

Working on The Dust Waltz has been one of the most enjoyable experiences in my career, simply because of how comfortable I feel in Sunnydale. I'm grateful for the opportunity to take Buffy, Willow, Xander, Angel, and Giles out for an evening stroll . . . we had a fine time. I hope you do, too.

Dan Brereton
July 1998

chapter 1

PROMENADE

Sunnydale High has a long-standing rule that any student caught abusing her Study Period risks detention.

...Buffy Summers, the school librarian, Rupert Giles, considers crossbow repair an integral area of study...

...at least when it comes to Buffy's best subject, Vampire Slaying.

STUPID, STUPID CROSSBOW!

THAT DOES IT, GILES!

I'M NOW OFFICIALLY QUITTING AFTERSCHOOL SLAYING AND JOINING THE MATH CLUB.

CLATTER

Later, at the only hangout in town, The Bronze...

UNCLE DOESN'T REALIZE IT, BUT I'VE BEEN STUDYING UP ON YOUR HOME TOWN. IT'S QUITE INFAMOUS.

WE'RE REAL BIG ON INFAMY HERE. YOU MIGHT SAY WE'RE NOTORIOUS FOR IT IN SUNNYDALE.

GILES STARTS TO CLEAR HIS THROAT AND COUGH WHENEVER I ASK HIM ABOUT THE 'PORTAL TO THE NETHERWORLD' YOU'RE SUPPOSED TO HAVE HERE...

...HAVE ANY OF YOU SEEN IT?

THAT'S JUST BABY STUFF THEY TELL YOU TO SCARE YOU INTO EATING YOUR PEAS AND CARROTS.

LIKE WHEN YOU'RE, YOU KNOW, A BABY. BABIES DON'T EVEN BELIEVE THAT STUFF.

I SEE...

WOULD YOU LIKE TO DANCE WITH ME, XANDER?

"LIKE" ISN'T A STRONG ENOUGH WORD FOR IT!

OH, SHE'S SO CRAFTY. WENT RIGHT FOR THE WEAK LINK IN THE CHAIN.

MEN ARE SO WEAK. AFTER A FEW SLOW SONGS, SHE'LL HAVE XANDER SHOWING HER WHERE WE BURIED THE MASTER'S BONES...

...NOT TO MENTION HELL-MOUTH.

WE NEED TO HAVE A NICE LONG TALK WITH HIM LATER, ABOUT GIRLS AND HOW THEY BEND YOUNG BOYS TO THEIR WILL WITH SORCEROUS POWERS ...WHAT AM I SAYING?

BUFFY! THOSE ARE TRADE SECRETS!

chapter 2

MOON
dANCE

BUMMER. I GUESS WE WON'T BE HAVING ON OF THOSE NEXT SPRING INSTEAD OF THE PROM.

NO, IT'S STRICTLY AN EVENT TO BE AVOIDED-- CANCELLED ENTIRELY, IN FACT.

IT CULMINATES WITH THE OPENING OF THE HELLMOUTH.

LET ME GUESS~THEY'RE NOT ALL GOING TO JUMP IN AT THE END ARE THEY, LIKE A "LET'S-THROW-EVERYBODY-INTO-THE-POOL" KIND OF THING?

IT'S *NOT* THAT KIND OF PARTY, BUFFY. IT'S, UM, MORE OF A SUMMONING.

MAJOR BUMMER.

WHAT EXACTLY ARE THEY PLANNING ON SUMMON-ING?

I WISH I KNEW.

CONSIDERING LILITH'S POWER, IT COULD BE SOMETHING, SHALL WE SAY, FORMIDABLE.

THE dUST WALTZ

dan BRERETON

Dan Brereton was not always a suave comics creator. In fact, he used to be a foolhardy little kid with very little common sense who used to catch snakes for fun. Today, he is a self-professed monster lover, toy geek, and crime-fiction fan. The three pursuits have found their way into nearly every damn thing he's ever done in comics. Dan has enjoyed critical success in the field of comics illustration as well as distinguished himself as one of a crop of new writers in comics with his own brand of Monster Noir projects, *Nocturnals: Black Planet* (coming in October of '98 as a trade paperback from Oni Press) and *Nocturnals: Witching Hour* (Dark Horse). He's also collaborated with comics greats Walter Simonson and Howard Chaykin and is currently working with rocker Rob Zombie on a new comics project, once again involving his Nocturnals. His creator-owned big-monster epic, *Giantkiller,* debuts in the spring of '99. He lives with his three-child circus act and their fish, Flame, near Lake Tahoe, California.

hector gomez

Born in Argentina in 1953, graduated architect Hector Gomez moved to Brazil in 1976, where he lives today. He has worked as an advertising illustrator, and his painted work has been exhibited in a number of art galleries in both Brazil and Argentina. Hector's work has been published by a slew of Brazilian and American publishers, including *Paranoia* for Malibu, *Battlestar Galactica* for Maximum Press, and *What If* for Marvel. After a two-year absence from comics, where he found work as an art director for a webpage-design company, *Buffy* is Hector's return to the American comic-book scene.

sandu FLOREA

Between his Tibetan yoga and steady diet of ice cream, inking extraordinare Sandu Florea has made a name for himself working on some of the top books in the industry. Besides current stints on *Blade* and *Conan*, Sandu's talents have graced the pages of *Captain America, Thor,* and *The Avengers.* The work on *Buffy the Vampire Slayer* is well suited for Sandu, considering he was born and raised in a small mountain village in Transylvania, a mere ten miles from Dracula's castle!

All publications are available through most good bookshops or direct from our mail-order service at Titan Books. For a free
graphic-novels catalogue or to order, telephone 01858 433 169 with your credit-card
details or contact Titan Books Mail Order, Bowden House, 36 Northampton Road,
Market Harborough, Leics, LE16 9HE, quoting reference BRS/GN.